Dear Tzio

I HOPE YOU LIKE THIS
BOOK, KHISON WAS OUR
NEIGHBOUR IN NEW YORK.

HAPPY BIRTHDAY
WE LOVE YOU LOTS.
AUNTY MINERLA, CHRLSS, CONSTANST
ELLA

29 DECEMBER 2021

Happy Birthday 2020!

— Khisin

KHISON IS HAVING COMPANY

written by
Allison &
Khison Dunn

Dear reader,

After giving birth to Khison and starting my own business as a home organizer, I began to experience the struggle most parents have; keeping the house tidy and organized while still allowing my little munchkin to run around and play. It wasn't until I saw my son repeating my organizing routines that I realized the value of including my son in the tidying process. I managed to make it fun, not a chore, and as a result, we both enjoy tidying and organizing together. My hope is that this story will inspire other families with children to use cleanup time as a bonding experience and that they will find a new way to discover joy! I hope that when you read this book you will see the mess that your child created while playing not as a reason to be stressed, but as an opportunity to spark joy by cleaning up together.

Sincerely,

ALLISON & KHISON DUNN

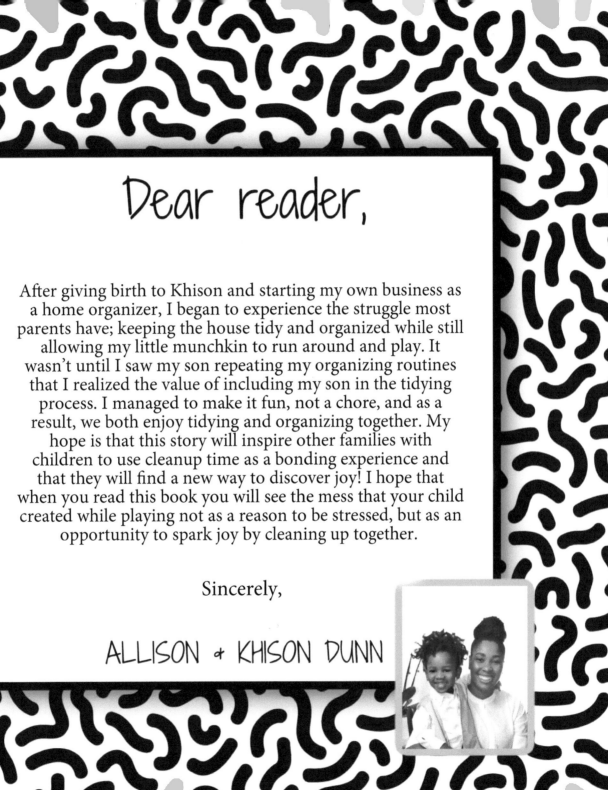

The book is dedicated to my son for inspiring me to tell his story—A.D.

KHISON IS HAVING COMPANY

written by
Allison &
Khison Dunn

Khison opened his eyes, confused. The last thing he remembered was playing with his toys. How had he ended up in his bed? Stretching, Khison looked out the window.

It was a new day! That could only mean one thing. His friends would be coming over soon to play soccer!

Khison jumped out of bed. But as he
stepped onto the floor—*ouch!*

He stepped on a toy dinosaur.

Khison looked around his room. It was a mess!
Khison hung his head. How was he going to have a play date with his
room looking like this? He knew he had to get it cleaned—*and fast.*
But the more Khison thought about cleaning, the more anxious he
became. The mess was just too big.

Khison knew he needed help, and he knew just who to call: his mom. Mom was great at cleaning messes. Everything in their house was perfectly organized. In fact, Mom's job was teaching people how to organize!

"**Mom!**" he yelled with all his might!

"Good morning, Khison," Mom said when she came in. "You were sure having fun last night! When I came in to say good night, I found you asleep in a pile of toys. I had to scoop you into bed!"

Khison smiled weakly.

"What's wrong?" Mom asked.

Khison gestured at the mess around him. "My friends will be here soon, and I really want my room to be neat. But I don't know where to start!"

Mom smiled. "Well, where do we always start? With your bins, right?" Khison nodded and ran to get his bins. He laid them out next to each other on the floor. Just seeing them made him start to feel better.

"Good," Mom said.

"Now what do we do?" Khison asked.

"We sing our song!" he shouted at last.

Khison loved singing the cleanup song. It always put him in a happy mood. "Let's sing it together, Mom!"

"Clean up, clean up, everybody clean up.
Clean up, clean up, let's get organized!
Pick up all your toys, put them in the bins.
Put the books on the bookshelf, and make a pretty rainbow."

"That's right, Khison!" Mom said. "You make me so proud!"
Mom took Khison's hand and the two sang the cleaning song and danced around the room. Soon they were both in a great mood!

As Khison danced, he grabbed a toy and put it in one pile. He put a book in another pile. In no time, he and his mom had made lots of little piles for toys and books.

Khison packed all the items into the right bins, and put the books on the bookshelf in rainbow order. Then Mom helped him make his bed, get dressed, and put away his pajamas.

Finally, everything was perfect.
"That was so fun, Mom!"
Khison chanted. "And now
everything is organized just the
way I like it!"
"I am so proud of you, Khison,"
said Mom. "I think you're ready
for that playdate!"

With his room clean, Khison and Mom went to relax for a few minutes.
Mom was telling Khison a story when, suddenly, he remembered
something.

"My soccer ball!"
Khison said.
"We're supposed to play
today, but where is it?"

Khison searched his toy bin. He looked under the bed. His soccer ball was nowhere in sight!

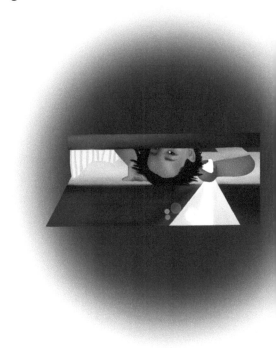

Just then, Khison heard the doorbell ring. His friends where there!
Khison ran to let them in. "Come on, let's go play in my room!" he said.

"Wow! Your room is so clean and organized, Khison!" Samantha said.

Zac nodded. "My room is so messy. My toys are all over the floor."

Khison grinned. "I can show you how to clean up if you want. I can even teach you my favorite clean-up song. It always gets me in the mood to clean."

Khison and his friends played and had fun in his room. When they were done, Khison stood to put a toy away in his closet. But as he opened it . . . "Hey! My soccer ball!" Khison said. Then he started to laugh. It was right where it belonged. He had never thought to check there!

Khison grabbed the ball and the three friends started playing soccer.

A few minutes later, Khison's mom poked her head in and asked if they wanted a snack. She showed them three ice cream cones—Khison's favorite.

As she was giving the kids the treat, Mom whispered in Khison's ear, "This s for a job well done this morning."

Khison grinned. He was happy to get ice cream, but he was even happier to ave everything back where it belonged!

Khison cleaned up, and you can, too. Follow the cleaning checklist to make sure that everything is put away properly.

Clean Your Room!

☐ Make my bed

☐ Fold my clothes

☐ Put dirty clothes in laundry basket

☐ Put my shoes on the shoe rack

☐ Organize my toys in bins

☐ Sweep or vacuum my room

Good Job!

CPSIA information can be obtained
at www.ICGtesting.com
Printed in the USA
BVHW022223240720
583893BV00008B/16